nch

od — two w

Nature Storybook

WALKER BOOKS

To Matthew Wallace K.W.

---

*To everyone who loves bears
and works to protect them* B.F.

*The publishers would like
to thank Dr Christopher Servheen
of the University of Montana for
his help and advice.*

First published 1994 by Walker Books Ltd
87 Vauxhall Walk, London SE11 5HJ

This edition with CD published 2009

10 9 8 7 6 5 4 3 2 1

Text © 1994 Karen Wallace
Illustrations © 1994 Barbara Firth

The right of Karen Wallace and Barbara Firth to be identified
as author and illustrator respectively of this work has been
asserted by them in accordance with the Copyright, Designs
and Patents Act 1988

This book has been typeset in Sabon

Printed in China

British Library Cataloguing in Publication Data:
a catalogue record for this book is available from the
British Library

ISBN 978-1-4063-1821-0

www.walkerbooks.co.uk

The bears in this book are black bears. This is the name of their species, but black bears are not always black. They can be reddish, silver, yellow, light brown or dark brown. Black bears are shy and good-natured animals, and they live in the forests of North America.

Bears in the Forest

Written by
Karen Wallace

WALKER BOOKS
AND SUBSIDIARIES
LONDON · BOSTON · SYDNEY · AUCKLAND

Illustrated by
Barbara Firth

Deep in a cave,
a mother bear sleeps.
She is huge and warm.
Her heart beats slowly.
Outside it is cold
and the trees are
covered in snow.
Her newborn cubs
are blind and tiny.
They find her milk
and begin to grow.

Bears sleep through the winter months.

A mother bear's cubs are usually born during her winter sleep.

Snow slips from
the trees and melts
on the ground.
The ice has broken
on the lake. Mother
bear wakes. Her long
sleep is over. She leads
her cubs down to
the lake shore.
She slurps and slurps
the freezing water.

Adult bears are very thirsty when they first leave their dens.

Young cubs are still drinking their mother's milk.

Leaves burst from their
buds. There are frogs'
eggs in the lake. Mother
bear snuffs the air for
strange smells, listens
for strange sounds.
Her cubs know
nothing of the forest.
This is their first spring.
Mother bear must
take care.

A mother bear brings up her cubs all by herself.

Bears are good mothers and protect their cubs fiercely.

11

The summer sun is hot.
Mother bear sits in
a tree stump. Angry bees
buzz around her head,
and stolen honey drips
from her paws.

Bears love honey.

They will rob a bees' nest even if the stings make them bawl with pain.

Her two skinny bear cubs
wrestle in the long grass.
They squeal like little boys
and roll over and over
away from their mother.
Mother bear growls.

Young bears grow quickly.

They are often quite thin during the early part of their first summer.

Come back! There are
dangers in the forest!
Her cubs do not hear her.
Mother bear snorts.
She is angry.
She strides across
the meadow and
whacks them with
a heavy paw.

Bears growl, whine, whinny, sniff, snuff, snort and bawl.

Bears are excellent climbers.

Two frightened bear cubs scramble
up the nearest tree. Mother bear waits
below, still as a statue, listening
to the forest. When she feels safe,
she will call her cubs down.
Mother bear must take care.

They can jump from high branches, too, and land unhurt.

Soon the days grow shorter
and squirrels start to hide acorns.
Bushes are bright with berries.
Seed pods flutter to the ground.
Winter is coming. Mother bear
and her cubs eat everything
they can find.

Bears eat grass shoots, mice, insects, fish, berries, nuts, seeds and honey.

In the autumn they eat as much as they can to prepare them for their winter sleep.

Icy winds blast the forest.
Mother bear plods through the snow.
Her cubs are fat. Their fur is thick.
She chooses a shelter that is dark and
dry, where they will sleep through
the long winter months.

During her winter sleep,

a bear's temperature drops and her heartbeat slows down.

When spring has
woken the bears again,
mother bear leads her cubs to the river.
She follows a trail worn deep in the ground.
Hundreds of bears have walked this way before her.

Bears use old bear trails whenever they can.

Bears leave their claw marks on trees, as messages to other bears.

The river runs deep and fast.
Mother bear wades in.
Soon a silver trout
flashes in her jaws.
The cubs are hungry.
They wade into
the river and catch
their own fish.

Bears are strong swimmers, and clever at catching fish.

Some time during their second summer,

Mother bear gobbles berries.
Her cubs are playing where
she can't see them.
They are almost grown.
Soon they will leave her.

Mother bear has taught them
everything she knows.

bear cubs leave their mother to find territories of their own.

Index

Look up the pages to find out about these bear things. Don't forget to look at both kinds of words: this kind and *this kind.*

Praise for Nature Storybooks...

"For the child who constantly asks How? Why?
and What For? this series is excellent."
The Sunday Express

"A boon to parents seeking non-fiction picture books to read
with their children. They have excellent texts
and a very high standard of illustration to go with them."
The Daily Telegraph

"As books to engage and delight children, they work superbly.
I would certainly want a set in any primary
classroom I was working in."
Times Educational Supplement

"Here are books that stand out from the crowd,
each one real and individual in its own right and
the whole lot as different from most other series non-fiction
as tasty Lancashire is from processed Cheddar."
Books for Keeps

Find notes for teachers about how to use Nature Storybooks in the classroom at
www.walkerbooks.co.uk/naturestorybooks

Nature Storybooks support KS 1-2 Science